To my children
and grandchildren ...
I love you
to the moon and back.

Cover design by Melanie Regier

Book design and layout by Melanie Regier

ISBN: 978-0-692-50606-6

Library of Congress Control Number: 2015914997

Printed in the United States of America by Mennonite Press, Inc., Newton, KS

www.mennonitepress.com

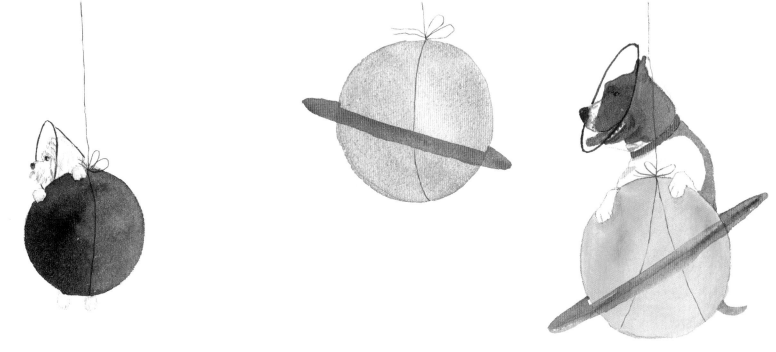

KIBBY is an ordinary, adorable dog that experienced something we all experience at one point in our lives...Rejection.

Along his journey he discovered things that will inspire children to accept who they are and accept others who are different. He learned the importance of not judging others for the way they look. When Kibby had to wear " the cone of shame", due to stitches, he truly experienced rejection. Children were reluctant to touch or get near him. During his walks, other dogs on the street ignored him. He was an unhappy dog and really disliked wearing the cone!

Kibby's real life experience inspired me to write this beautifully illustrated picture book. Even though Kibby is a dog, he feels and thinks just like we do. I want to convey the message to children, that it's okay to be different! My hope is that children celebrate similarities in each other, rather than notice the differences.

Celebrate being unique!
With Kibby Kisses, X X

Andrea

My name is Kibby.

I'm a miniature labradoodle.

I was born on St. Patrick's Day.
Life is wonderful!

I'm a
happy dog!

I love my adventurous walks in my neighborhood.
I watch the squirrels run around me.
I listen to the birds chirping. I let other dogs sniff me.

I am good friends with the dogs in my neighborhood. They give me lots of kisses.

Car rides are a special treat.

I get to stick my head out. I can see everything around me. I love the wind in my face.

People in other cars smile and wave at me.

They say, "What a cute dog!"

The children
in my neighborhood
play games with me.

I love it!

I am a happy dog!

I kiss
all the
kids!

One day, I had to visit the doctor at the veterinary clinic. I really liked the vet, especially because I got yummy treats! I saved up lots of kisses for the doctor too!

I needed stitches for a small cut
on one of my paws.

The doctor put a plastic cone-shaped
object around my head, so I wouldn't
chew on my stitches.

I didn't like the plastic cone!

It was different.

It bothered me.

I was a sad dog!

When I got home, I tried to

eat, drink, sleep, and play with my toys,

but it was so very hard to do anything

with that darn plastic cone

around my head!

I had to keep

the plastic cone

on my head

for 2 weeks!

It was a really long time.

I was a sad dog!

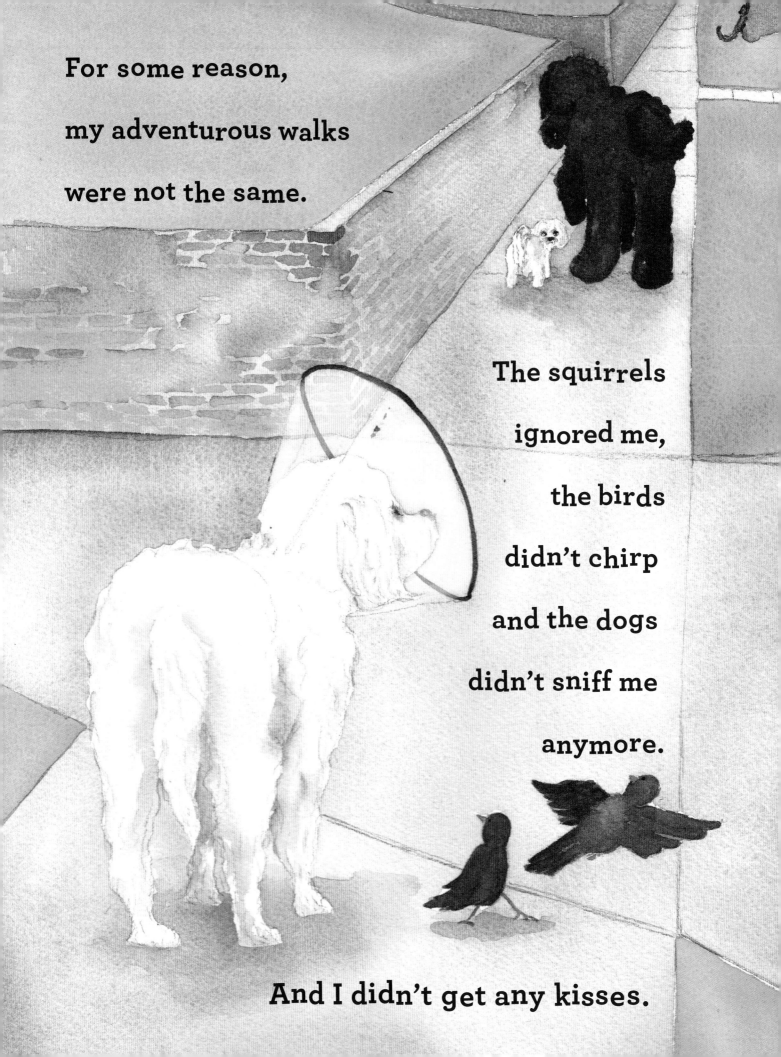

For some reason, my adventurous walks were not the same.

The squirrels ignored me, the birds didn't chirp and the dogs didn't sniff me anymore.

And I didn't get any kisses.

My car rides were not the same either.

People in other cars would laugh at me.

They said, "look at that dog!"

The children in my neighborhood didn't want to play games with me! I think they were afraid of me! I was a sad dog!

I couldn't do any of the

fun things I used to do.

Life wasn't so wonderful!

I was being rejected

because people thought I was now different.

My life was not the same anymore.

I lost my fun,

playful spirit.

One night......

I had this amazing dream!

I went to outer space. I saw

lots of dogs wearing plastic

cones on their heads just like

me! I saw many kinds of dogs.

Big

and

LITTLE

dogs.

And the dogs were happy!

And I didn't stand out.

I wasn't the only one who had a

plastic cone around his head!

Outer space was fun!

No one judged me or laughed at me.

All the dogs treated me the same.

I got lots of **sniff** sniff sniffs

I learned to eat,
drink, sleep and play
with the plastic cone around
my head by watching
the other dogs.

I was a happy dog!

All of a sudden...

I woke up.

I found myself back in my bed.

It was only a dream.

I was a sad dog!

Again!

I wanted to be back in space with the

other dogs, who were just like me.

No one would ignore me.

And no one would laugh at me.

And everyone would play games with me.

And everyone would

sniff
sniff
sniff
me!

These past 2 weeks

were hard for me.

It seemed like years.

I got used to the

way things were.

I accepted it.

Today, I went to
visit my doctor again.
She checked
my stitches to see
if they had healed.

The doctor said that I had healed nicely.

She said the plastic cone could come off. Yippie!!

I was a happy dog!

When I got home,
I went for my
adventurous walks
in my neighborhood.

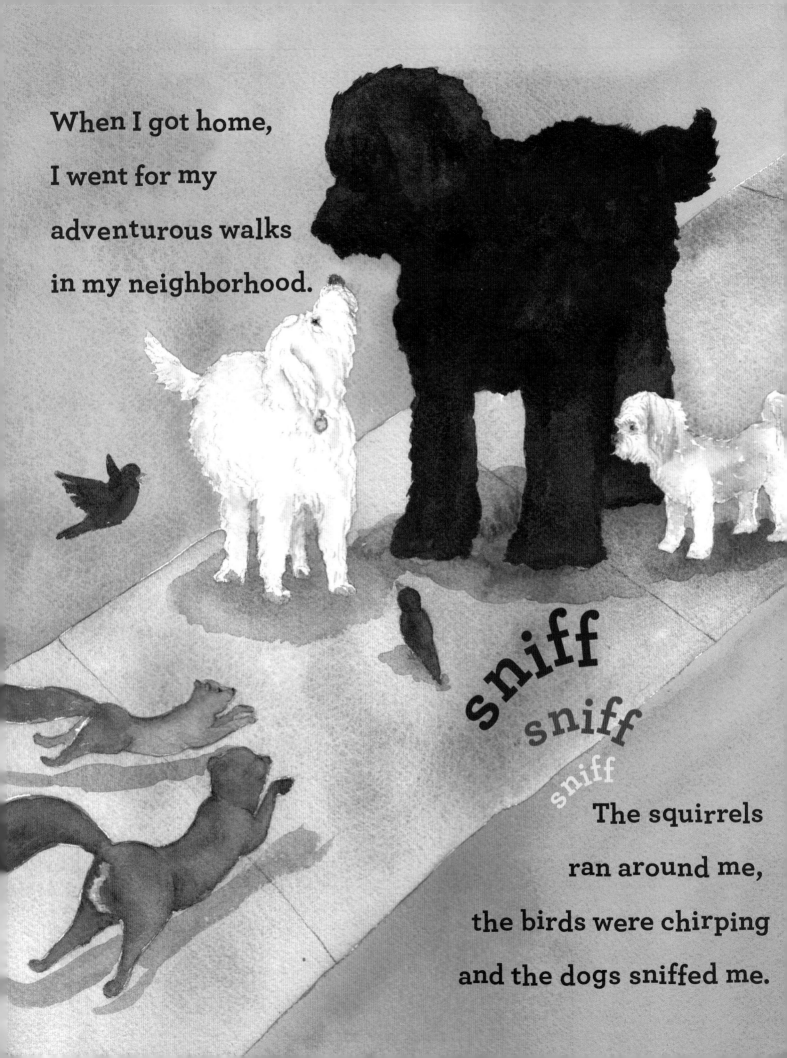

sniff
sniff
sniff

The squirrels
ran around me,
the birds were chirping
and the dogs sniffed me.

I went for a ride in the car.
I stuck my head out so I could see
everything around me.

People in other cars smiled at me
and said, "what a cute dog!"

The children
in my neighborhood
played games
with me!

And I was
so delighted!
I was a happy dog!
I loved and
kissed everyone!

One day, on one of my adventurous walks,
I saw a dog in my neighborhood wearing a
plastic cone around his head.

He looked like a sad dog!

So, I went over to the dog.

I gave him a nice **sniff**
sniff
sniff

He was very friendly.

He gave lots of kisses too.

I remembered how I felt when

I had the plastic cone

around my head.

I remembered how everyone

ignored me. I remembered

how I didn't fit in.

I remembered how I was a sad dog!

And I didn't want this dog to feel

the same way I did.

I hoped the dog would have an

amazing dream, like me.

I hoped he would dream he saw

lots of dogs in space,

wearing plastic cones on their

heads, just like him!

And no one would judge him.

And no one would laugh at him.

And he would be in a wonderful

place where everyone was treated the same.

And then he would be

a happy dog!

Flip this page to see real photos of Kibby and his friends!